N.L. Tim

Kevin C. McLeod, MD

WestBow
PRESS®
A DIVISION OF THOMAS NELSON
& ZONDERVAN

WestBow Press books may be ordered through booksellers or by contacting:

WestBow Press
A Division of Thomas Nelson & Zondervan
1663 Liberty Drive
Bloomington, IN 47403
www.westbowpress.com
844-714-3454

ISBN: 978-1-6642-9988-7 (sc)
ISBN: 978-1-6642-9989-4 (e)

Library of Congress Control Number: 2023908995

Print information available on the last page.

WestBow Press rev. date: 05/22/2023

Contents

CHAPTER I

N.L. HELPS MAMA

One event for sure sealed all the deals, savored by all, brought rapture down to earth, and just for moments raised lives up to par with royalty. It was that sumptuous repast at noon on Sunday after church. No one along the meandering Cat Claw Creek could spread a table with farm fresh goodness or more bouquet style than Mrs. Ella McLeod. If fresh kinfolk unexpectedly rolled up in the front yard, got out, went over the salutations, and gave hugs and handshakes, she had already bounced out the kitchen door, neck-twisted an ol' hen, plucked feathers, washed, chopped, floured, and had those pieces in the frying oil afore those folk ever stepped near the table.

She was not just fast, but she was good fast—smooth! She could run a fifty-yard dash holding a tray of nitroglycerin bottles and win— and you would have never heard a *kaboom*. Years later, they would say when the flash from San Benito, Texas, Bobby Morrow, won track sprint gold medals for ACC and America in the 1956 Olympics that he could have done better if he just tried harder. Truth was, for him, just like for Mrs. Ella, not a single sway of wasted motion, without sound combustion, in an all-consuming fire leaving no soot, ash, residue—top tuned on all cylinders an apparition of silk and smoke—then *poof*—gone!

However, this was a Saturday noon before all the ruckus of the Sunday, when a palpable quietness infused the house. Pete, up in the front room, would take boots off and stretch out on the couch for a well-deserved fifteen to thirty minute honest to goodness nap. The older boys would relax too, going out to the barn for small talk on the hay bales and playing mumblety-peg with pocket knives.

Mrs. Ella had N.L. with her for kitchen duty. She (and he) were going to be fixing up her famous banana pudding. N.L. was excited 'cause Aunt Toadie had just given Ella the new miracle machine for the kitchen called an automatic blender. He had seen it in operation, how the beater blades spindled into the top housing and you could dial in the rotation speeds. It fascinated him that the tines just barely missed jamming into each other. He knew at any minute they were going to have beaters gnarled into a metallic twisted twined jabber-jaw mess.

With fixings laid out, she sat N.L. down, edged up against the table with a large mixing bowl in his lap. There was the Karo syrup, evaporated milk, melted butter, sugar, eggs, flour, vanilla wafers, and bananas would come later. This was mixing time. He just knew that at any moment Mrs. Ella was going to whirl up the magic marvel. Instead, she handed him a large wooden spoon and instructed him to *slowly* add in the ingredients and stir. She sounded out the word, "S-L-O-W-L-Y."

Exclaimed the startled N.L., "But Mom, what about your new egg beatin' machine?"

She slid over next to him, looked around, and whispered, "I don't trust that thing, churning so fast like that sure's to make for touch pudding—I want it smooth blended, not whirlwinded like a tornado would do. Why, have you ever seen what things looking like after a twister plowed through—not for my pudding!"

N.L. minded and slowly added and stirred, and added and stirred. It was empty church-house quiet. The only sound was the numbing drone of the small kitchen fan. Even though this was west Texas, a zephyr-like breeze from the Aegean Sea calmly ruffled N.L.'s hair. He dozed, stirred a little, dropped his chin, stirred, and then really dozed with arm bent on the table and his head resting there. He had a speckle of flour on his nose from a previous itch and scratch.

Course Mrs. Ella was aware of the drifter and softly removed the bowl and finished the mixings. After a while, N.L. stretched and stood up to stretch some more. Blinking and yawning again, he saw the bowl before him. "Mama, reckon I finished that afore I rested a little?" He was scratching his head now with prideful motions that he really had helped out his mama. Still, he was a little quizzical about his overall contribution to the concoction.

Next day at dessert serving time, out came the complete goodness of Ella's Nanner Pudding. Of course, once Pete had finished his bowl he winked and said, "Mama, that was laripen-sure!"

Homer asked, "Hey Mom, did you use the new egg beater that Aunt Toadie gave ye?"

Mrs. Ella just smiled and said, "That's a wondrous machine."

Homer replied, "Sure is, and you can make everything so much faster and better!"

Mrs. Ella kinda tilted her head, saying, "Faster probably for sure, now better—I think the proof to that is still in the pudding."

N.L. said, "Know what I would call this now Mama? Nappa pudding!"

"Dat's right son, we could for sure." She laughed.

Homer asked, "What?" Looking directly at N.L., he said, "Whata you know about it anyway?"

N.L. replied, "Reckon I could fix it up in my sleep—right, Mama?" From then on, just between her and him, if any reference came up concerning her Cat Claw Creek world-famous banana pudding, they'd look at each other, saying, "nappa pudding!"

CHAPTER II

N.L. GETS DA CRITTER

This was a strange time along Cat Claw Creek when most everybody was away. Pete had some of the boys up to Roscoe for a cattle sale and the girls had gone to Ethel's to start work on their Easter dresses. Mrs. Ella and N.L. had the house to themselves. It was surprisingly pleasant without doors being jarred open, creaking, or slamming, and without being yelled at after every minute. Mrs. Ella had a dandy supper of fried chicken, sweet potatoes, and her gold-medal-winning bronze-crusted rolls with fresh cow butter. After the meal came a lazy time with N.L., mostly listening to the radio with his dog Snappy. A more contented couple wrapped paw and palm there never was.

Finally, west Texas got dark enough for bedroll call. The boy and dog, both scratching over themselves in a most satisfied way, slowly shuffled up the steps to the loft. "Night Mama—love you," he sallied back.

He got a similar message coming back up. "You, too, sweeties! Sleep tight. Don't let the bed bugs bite!"

All was well until somewhere, from the depths of darkness, came this commotion. Snappy was downstairs pitching yelps and sniffing, clawing like trying to dig through the baseboards. Mrs. Ella came rushing in, tying her gown up. A burr-eyed boy half stumbled down the stairs. "What is it Maw?"

Surmised Mrs. Ella, "Likely he's smelled some critter up under the house."

"I'll get Daddy's gun!" exclaimed N.L.

Said Ella, "Best not. You get a gunnysack and Papa's long walking stick. I'll get the lantern. We can likely chase a varmint up out there, or we'll get no rest tonight."

They went out back with the attack dog, stick, sack, and lantern. As N.L. opened the under porch door, his mama said, "Now if'n you see white on black—some ol' skunk—why you skittle right back out here!"

Dark had really stacked itself in shades under there as Snappy left the little arch of golden light and disappeared barking somewhere up ahead. That was when N.L. first realized he had an organ transplant for where his throat use to be his heart was striking along at snare-drum speed. He crawled along, light in one hand, pole and sack in the other, wishing that Snappy could chase whatever it was out some side hole. He saw Snappy's tail whipping good enough to churn butter, and the meter intensified.

That is when N.L. saw the evil glaring straight back at him—yellow eyes! Then a yellow double row of pincher teeth snapped open with a hiss. It rattled his bones, and in so doing he dropped the stick and sack. What happened next was a sure mystery. Snappy, with cautious lunges, moved to the side and then behind this creature, and N.L. could not back up quickly enough on his all fours. This frenzy started directly for him, spitting, snapping, snarling, yapping, all roller-balling his way. The gunnysack lay open mouthed, and in the half a millisecond, the *thing* darted directly in there to get away from Snappy. N.L. could barely think, but he braced the stick over the sack's mouth end and bore down. In the bottom of that sack was a twisting, turning, and true Tasmanian. But N.L. got the top knotted around. He had his captive!

"Good boy, Snappy!" exclaimed Mrs. Ella and Snappy was leaping around like an Olympic champion.

Asked Mrs. Ella, "Why son, what on earth do we have got in that?"

"Not sure at all, Maw, it happened so fast!"

They talked all excited about what to do next, deciding this evening had already had enough action. They would put the critter, still inside the sack, into an empty barrel drum and shut the lid down. Said Mr. Ella, "At dawn's first glow, reckon we better have Pete's gun, just in case, afore we open that lid!"

"Right Mama!" returned N.L.

Early next morning, they went outside to the drum. N.L. slowly slid the lid back and they both heard all this hissing coming from the bottom. Slowly he peeked over the rim, careful not to get his head out over that opening more than necessary. Snappy was no help now as he charged around the base and between their legs, which they might need for a quick getaway.

Asked Mrs. Ella, "What ya thinking, son? See it can you?"

N.L. did see *it*. "Maw, it's a possum- cept it's a mother with babies!" Sure enough, still snarling and laying on her back was the mama with nine babies squirming on her belly for breakfast.

All Mrs. Ella could say was, "Land of Goshen! Don't that beat all! Now here's what we gotta do. I will keep Snappy inside while you cap this lid back and take this barrel away, I mean away out in the field—just tip it over and you come running back home, all right?"

When Pete and the boys got home, they got to hear about all the wild kingdom. Homer seemed to be one most astonished. Said N.L., "Yep, Snappy and me went up under there—no fears—caught all *ten* of them opossums all by ourselves!"

Said Homer, "Now hold the phone." He looked at Mrs. Ella and she nodded.

"The boy's telling you the God's truth. It was *ten*!"

Homer, scratching the cap on his head, said, "Now I know you call ten sheep a flock, ten fish a school, and ten lions a pride, but what in tarnation do you call ten possums?"

Pete put his head back and started to laugh. "Okay, I believe I've got a handle on this now." Putting a hand on Homer's shoulder, he said, "I think you'd call that a family—a passel. One mama and nine pups! Jills and joeys." He shot a wink at N.L.

CHAPTER III

N.L. and the Case of
the Mad Hatter

In the 1920s, who would have considered that someday you would take a four-foot-long windmill blade for pumping water and expand it out to ninety feet to turbine electricity. Beyond Cat Claw Creek on the mesa south of the McLeod old home place is now a bristle of rotators up on towers, whirring for all to see, trying to break the roots off and have the whole cap rock will lift up and go skyward. That constant wind with its blustering billows accounts for the energy of this story.

After school this day, N.L. and friend Toby spent their last nickels on a large soda drink at the drug store and had the mid-tummy fizzy fuzzy feel along with light-headedness. As they shuffled out, some important men across the street were strolling beyond the bank's front doors. A kipper gust suddenly whooshed down Main Street and in the blink of a dusty eye, three men's hats skated off, rolling down the road.

The two bowler hats were quickly chased down by the scampering boys, but that Stetson was galloping away. "Boys!" yelled one of the men, pointing a big finger at the disappearing head gear. With full soda stomachs, they took off, thinking at first it would be easy to just run up on it—but that wind toyed with them like a cat with a twine ball.

N.L. and Toby crashed into each other just as their outstretched hands barely missed a mutual grab. Toby fell but N.L. stumbled on, regaining balance. He could just barely hear the men behind him yelling encouragement. The hat landed on the crossroad upside down, and just as N.L. was approaching it, a second blustering wind flicked it up into flight.

This time the hat kited up twenty-five feet into a main stream, twirling but maintaining a captured upright position with N.L. running under it. Across the back yard, Mrs. Fowler's chickens were being scattered with boisterous cackling in all directions as the hat and N.L. dashed through. Next, it was across Mr. Bullington's cow lot, with the hat bouncing over the bovine backs pinball fashion.

The hat escaped on its own wings out over Mr. Sloan's cotton field, zigging and zagging. All the while, N.L. was pumping his legs to stay caught up. Just then, a lull seemed to sigh. The hat was going to abandon its getaway spirit and nestle down on the cotton balls, and N.L. was going to snatch hold of that big brim.

Just then, out of nowhere came the strangest encounter yet. It was the true critter herself but only in west Texas: a tower topping fifty-foot-high dust devil! She was a perfectly twirling funnel, complete with brown dust, cotton leaves, and now a Stetson hat riding her out like Pecos Bill. The hat inside the funnel went up, up, up, then shot like Spindle Top out the top of the derrick. N.L.'s legs could carry him no farther and he stood blinded by dust as the wind devil twirled out its short life. Looking up into the sky, he tried to shield his eyes but could not see the hat anywhere.

Then something thumped his head, then his shoulder, and fell across his feet as if in total surrender now from its escape: the Stetson! Before another thing could happen, reaching down with both hands, he grasped the brim on the hat without a mark anywhere, just like being presented out of the hatbox. The three men were waiting out on the road, having witnessed the whole event in wonderment. There was a chorus of handshakes, big smiles, and back patting for this high-priced hat rescue. Said the gentleman who now reached for the hat, "Son, that was quite a stampede and you corralled it down. I'd be sure sore to lose this 10X beaver Philadelphia-made Stetson!"

N.L. was smiling too. It was one of the hardest scampers he'd ever been on and he was tickled to have it resolved. Said the Stetson man before turning to leave, "Hey, here's a half dollar for your next round of sodas and for all your effort. So to speak, my hat's off to you."

CHAPTER IV

TALE OF A TAIL

Brisk autumn breezes now aligned with the pole star (so stated Mr. Pete) and brought a chill enough for goosebumps to appear for those on Cat Claw Creek. Neighbors, the Robinsons, always left this time of year for a week with their family, putting up a harvest. They had just acquired a new dog, a young Border collie just graduating from puppyhood, a new scholar in the bright, big world. They and Mr. Pete made an arrangement for N.L. to keep Buster during gathering time.

Boy and dog were instant pals, both knowing one was made for the other and vis-à-vis. They romped, chased, tussled, and wrestled in a way that only youth on youth could do. Buster followed N.L. to school every day, no matter how many sticks and rocks were thrown back his way. It was all a game. Then Buster would snooze, waiting down by the school steps to jog back home with N.L.

That Saturday, Mr. Pete gave N.L. the job of hatch splitting small wood for kindling. Out over the old stump, he gathered up to the task. Of course Buster was all over this new curious contest. N.L. would balance up a stick and Buster would knock it over or else mouth it and run off. Buster was even snatching on to his glove as he worked the hatchet

There was nothing else he could do but rope his most unwilling captive to the tree. O the yelping for freedom accompanied by yanks and twirls and tries to bite the leash. Now N.L. could ignore pitiful howling and got into the groove of uprighting, hatching, and stacking his every enlarging wood pile.

From the barn, he heard Mr. Pete holler, "How's it going out thar?"

N.L. half turned his head with hatchet headed down and it all happened so fast: flash of fur, he's off balance, hatchet is off target. In his escape, Buster had jumped over the stump and now a painful high-pitched *yelp* exploded and there on the stump was the twitching, bloody half tail end. Buster was spinning in the grass, whimpering and trying to get what remained of his tail in his mouth.

N.L. was shocked, sorrowful, and scared. In a flood of emotion, he dropped hatchet and ran to Buster. Tears blurred his vision as he tried to hug the dog. Then he saw Pete's boots standing next to him. N.L., on his knees, cradled Buster, who was licking the exposed flesh of his half tail and then the boy's face. N.L. did not want to look up and see disgust in his father's eyes.

Calmly, Mr. Pete spoke down to him. "I saw the whole thing son. You were doing your work, Buster got himself in the wrong spot—none's to blame."

Said N.L., "Can we put it back on, sew it back or something?"

"No," replied Pete, "reckon not. What's done is done. Could have been worse. Some dogs I've knowed lived whole lives without any tails. But here we will treat that wound." He turned to walk away to get some coal tar.

N.L. pleaded after him. "But what will the Robinsons think? Bet they'll hate me. Just look at this!"

They took Buster to the back porch and Mrs. Ella put on the salve: poultice of coal tar for the dog and a heartfelt hug for the boy. Buster moved about much more slowly that afternoon, always checking his half tail for changes. By the next morning, he was jogging around like half tails are just dandy.

Still, N.L. could not help but think the Robinsons would be rightfully angry for their altered dog. When the day came for he and Mr. Pete to walk Buster back home, he wished he could just watch the return from the safety of the road. When they got there, they went straight up on the porch and the Robinsons were joyous to see Buster but they sure needed some explanation.

Mr. Pete did all the talking as Buster just sat back on his haunches, ready for the story, and keeping time with his half tail. Said Pete in a straightforward manner, "N.L. and Buster sure got to be great pals, but on Saturday we had an accident. We're right sorry. We were chopping kindling and we had him tied up, but somehow he got loose of there and, as you can see, got the back end of his tail cut off and we will do anything you can think of to make amends."

Surprising to N.L., the Robinsons took the tail story in stride and gathered Buster into the house. N.L. and Mr. Pete started walking back home in a quiet spell. Finally, N.L. spoke up. "You didn't tell them about me. I is the one that chopped his tail half off—didn't I?"

Walking a little farther, Mr. Pete said, "Well son, I volunteered you to keep Buster without asking because I knew you'd do a best good job and you did—sure did. And when you were making kindling, you were working for me. I set you up there. When you are working together like that, anything that happens in an honest effort is my responsibility—yep. You swung the hatchet but *we* cut that dog's tail half off, okay?"

N.L. remembered that walk his whole life. On this road (and later on in life) his steps were a bit surer as he headed home, walking side by side with his father.

CHAPTER V

N.L. AND DAT BLACK CAT

Seems like in the late 1920s, as October waltzed in bringing crisp valley air, orange sunsets, and longer, trundled shadows, Cat Claw Creek had a last bout of arousal afore going dormant before winter. Often crowned also just above the ground was a huge blood moon.

Out from school, the boys had been talking about hexes and jinxes of bad luck that their Mexican friend called *mal ojo*—the evil eye. One had to be careful between that time of shadows not to be caught out in the gloom that had lurking spirits seeking those unaware.

Not that he believed in any of this hocus pocus, but there was nothing wrong with the rabbit's foot he had in his front pants pocket or the queen of hearts card in his breast pocket. Just to be on the safe side, up under the inside brim of his cap was a handmade copy of the title page of his mama's King James Bible.

Just a week away from Halloween, he was given the late afternoon task of staying after school to beat chalk dust out of the erasers. Mrs. Ella figured as much when N.L. did not pounce up on the front porch at the usual time. She called the school on the party line, asking N.L. not to come home until he had gone by the sale barn and picked up a bag of oats.

N.L. walked into the graying shadows of Mr. Benson's feed store and, without looking up, Mr. Benson pointed a finger backwards where to find the oats.

Thru a swing door, there was one weakening streak of sunlight beamed on the dusty floor, caught in between dim and darkness. Now just as N.L. was getting wide-eyed enough to see something, he really did see something. Right before him darted the blackest cat ever, arched back, claws, yellow eyes, fanged teeth, hissing and spitting like it had been scaled by Lucifer himself.

N.L. forgot his errand. He walked backwards, realizing the import of this evil specter. As he walked back, suddenly he bumped into a huge fleshy body. It was the owner, Mr. Benson. He asked, "What's taking you so long son? Didn't you get your oats?"

N.L. turned and looked a way up. "Well I—I was—well, but that black cat came after me!"

Mr. Benson let out a hoarse laugh. "You mean our barn cat? Why, she's as harmless as an old shoe unless you be rodent, then you'd hightail. She catches all the mice around here. Let me show you. Here Mystic, here puss-puss, here!"

From the dark depth of a bin strutted out the cat like she was modeling designer clothes, swaying and swishing right up to purr around Mr. Benson's leg.

Said Mr. Benson, "Now N.L., you got no fears about this little feline. She's been in the coal bin again hunting dem rodents. Why, looky here!" He picked her up and began dusting her fur. As he did, the black went to gray then to tabby until her true base broadcast through: she was pumpkin orange. N.L. realized he could breathe again. Then Mr. Benson gave him a piece of advice that he always remembered. "Nothing can scare you unless you scare yourself first!"

CHAPTER VI

N.L. AND HIS FIREFLIES

It being the beginning of June along Cat Claw Creek, with June bugs, of course, the days were just toast but with the sure promise of more sweltery times ahead. At dusk, the cooling skies seemed to silhouette into the shallows off the purple mesas behind McLeod Ranch.

Some of the kids finishing the day were skipping stones down by the creek as fireflies were just turning their tails up for competition with the twinkling stars. N.L.'s idea was to snag some of these nature's nightlights into a Mason jar with holes punched in the lid for air. None of the cousins seemed inclined to the task, allowing N.L. all the room he needed for hard working to and fro until he had about a dozen of the beaming bottoms—his lightning bugs—as he paraded back toward home.

Homer intercepted him at the porch. "Now what earthly good you're going to do with that?"

Responded N.L., "Why these could be a light for the whole evening—like a lantern!"

"Nay, you're just wasting your time, buddy-boy," said Homer as he shuffled off.

N.L. took his sparkling jar around back to show Mrs. Ella. She acknowledged his effort, saying, "Just don't bring them into the house, son. What you can do is run out to the bottom field and tell your Daddy it's supper time."

N.L. did not trust what might happen if he left his flashing jar lying about so, taking off in a jog, he just carried them along.

Mr. Pete was trying to finish this last strip before all the natural light was gone. He knew there was an old mesquite stump down there he needed to avoid—with a slight curse to himself that he had not a kerosene lamp. Just as N.L. was getting close, Mr. Pete jammed the tractor off and jumped sideways. If demon possession was legal in Taylor County, he would have had a supreme case. Slapping, twisting, turning, stumbling, Mr. Pete was sure in torture.

N.L. helped him up off the ground and they started running, knowing instinctively to get out of there. With some distance, Mr. Pete was feeling over his face; with hat, long shirt, overalls, gloves, and boots, the hornets could only get to his face and they had. Not being down to that far end of the field in a while, a wasp nest had built up in that old stump and when he ran over it, they came swarming. Mr. Pete sure thanked N.L. for helping him away from there. Mrs. Ella was all ready to hear telling of the hornet story as Mr. Pete's face was looking like Mr. Potato Head. They got him into the bedroom, taking his overalls off when he said, "My watch—my Dad's watch! It was in this pocket. Oh no, must of fell out down there!"

Said Mrs. Ella, "Don't mind that for now. You is all right is the main thing—long as you don't swell no more."

But Mr. Pete just sighed. "Yea, but that was the onlyest thing he could give me."

Returned Mrs. Ella, "Gonna be dark the whole night through. We got no lights to go down thar. We'll just wait for God breaking open his sun in the morning's.'

N.L. heard all this and remembered his jar was still down there. To get there, he would have to walk over charcoal ground sealed below by pitch black sky. He knew what he had to do and, without telling anybody, he sneaked away. As he got closer, he thought he saw a faint glow, then again a little sparkle, closer still a flicker, then *yes!*

Them buggers were still showing off their tail ends. He was so glad to find them all right. He really was not expecting anything else, *but* just as he turned, in the corner of his eye he thought he saw a glint, a reflection, a Tasman—he held his jar closer to the ground and slowly walked ahead thinking, *What about them hornets?* But there truly was something on the ground and he reached and grasped it.

Next morning, Mr. Pete was moving real slow and his face looked like a jigsaw puzzle but with pieces all in the wrong places. At the breakfast table, he had a little wheeze. When N.L. came in, with a little cough, Mr. Pete showed his gratitude. N.L. was carrying still that lightning bug Mason jar, which he never did get to show his dad last evening.

Homer spoke up. "Now don't be bothering him with that silly show-off thing. Besides, Mama told you to keep it out of here remember." N.L. paid him no mind, setting the jar down in front of Mr. Pete.

With nearly swollen shut eyes, Mr. Pete starred and blinked. "That's a nice bug collection you got there, son."

Mrs. Ella kindly reminded him, "I did say something 'bout you keeping that outside."

But N.L. just waited, until finally Mr. Pete, with a sure, fat-lipped smile exclaimed, "Wait, what, who, where, how, but (starting a tradition that is still employed today by any McLeod), my stars, Mama, comma here—looky this!"

Mrs. Ella saw and had a smile that could out beam a troop of glow bugs. It was Samuel David's watch.

Homer never did say anything to N.L. about his country-style illumination, but only sat there snookered, looking at his biscuit. Finally, he said, "Well, the train that just ran me over didn't even show any blinking lights."

CHAPTER VII

N.L.'s First Radio

Up on Cat Claw Creek back in 1920s, constant puffs of west Texas winds enhanced a silence that tassled over the land like a finely tailored scarf. The quiet was right up next to your cheek like an atmospheric earmuff, only spiritual, presenting a deep silence that went back thousands of years.

But times were changing things fast. Work crews, telephone lines, railroads, tractors, and mills, and still the ancient throwback could happen such that a voice could surf the breeze for a quarter mile and still be heard out of nowhere. Unseen from on high and transmitted all around them, radio waves were offering out of the box news and entertainment, and people were now in their parlors, adjusting knobs for their favorite shows.

Mrs. Ella had turned down a page in the Sears and Roebuck for a handsome box radio set and she already had a cleared-off spot. Nearly every day, Mrs. Ella would be caught looking there and then to him, with her always pleading face, thinking, *When, Pete, when?*

Now N.L.'s pals at school were all talking only about transistors—the small hand-held sets that could capture the air waves. The very idea of being right there in west Texas yet hearing across America or from all over the world tickled their ears and minds.

But who had the money for such a device? They pooled their resources and formed a co-op, a secret society for AMs and FMs. When they had enough of the group's money, they went to McAnn's Hardware Store for the buy. What they did not figure on was tax, so gathered around the checkout counter stood a glop of glum-faced boys. One minute you're on a roller coaster and just like that—*bam*—you're sitting on a tire swing.

Mr. McAnn saw all the chest fallingness and he said in a whisper, "Boys, if you won't say anything and not broadcast this about, so to speak, neither will I. We'll forget tax this one time, okay?" All chipper now, the boys made an arrangement: drawing straws, they would take turns—three days and nights, and then it passed to the next fellow and on down the line.

It just happened that N.L.'s straw was shortest of the bunch and his turn would not come until Thanksgiving week. When his time came around, up in the loft by himself, he hid the antenna line under his bed then up and out through the window. He was going to bust before he got the dials set and he could hear something—mostly Mexican music with fast Spanish speakers or a faint station out of Waco. However, he was proud at least just to know now that he was tuned into the *world*.

Thanksgiving came par excellence, with Mrs. Ella's fixings and Mr. Pete's roasted turkey hitting all spots. A lazy, grand slumberness pervaded the house. N.L. retired to the loft and, tucking his head under his pillow, he dared tune in his set. Suddenly, by the grace of God, the solar winds, the ionosphere, or something supersonic, came this clear-toned voice, just like he was sitting in the broadcast booth knee to knee to the announcer. In fact, it was the first broadcast ever on radio of college football and it was Texas versus Texas A&M.

So adroit was the imagery pictured in his head that at times it seemed like N.L. was running with the ball, and he could feel the tacklers and experience the pile-ups. His mind hung on every word, teams moving right to left, huddled up on field, gathered on the sidelines. He kept hearing about "the line of scrimmage," how there was a new one every play and that it even switched sides, and that the ball would be sitting on the hash mark until teams were ready. He was amazed by the maze of the game. He was completely enthralled because even though his body was in Trent, Texas, his heart, brain, mind, and soul were in College Station, Texas.

Next day, after a few chores, for lunch all the men and boys were fed first from the storehouse of yesterday's leftovers. Homer had somehow got his hands on the *Abilene Reporter News* newspaper and was sitting there firing off comments. When he got to the sports page, he said, "Texas busted the Aggies 19–17—hum, hum—must have been a safety there for a two-point win."

Unthinkingly, N.L. offered, "Could have been Texas had a missed extra point then kicked a field goal."

Uncle Bud (one of N.L.'s favorite uncles who brought him gum and spending nickels), who had listened to the game on his own radio, said, "N.L.'s right about that score and there at the end Texas stopped A&M on the one-yard line."

N.L. could not hold back. "Yes Uncle Bud, but with that big pile-up, it was more like the one-foot line!"

Uncle Bud was now laughing. "Yes boy, you're right again." Bud got a wink from Mr. Pete, who knew about N.L.'s transistor and was enjoying the banter.

Now with one eye over the top of his paper, Homer continued, "Says here Taylor and Wilkins scored touchdowns for Texas." He semi-closed the paper, listening for any corrective response and, when nothing was forthcoming, raised the paper back up.

N.L., almost to himself, cautiously let out, "Taylor yes, but not Wilkins. It was Williams the Texas quarterback." He calmly forked his next piece of ham.

Said Homer, slamming the paper shut, "And I suppose you got all this out of thin air?"

Then Mr. Pete said, with a slight nod to N.L., "Now Homer, that is the first thing you said right all day!"

CHAPTER VIII

N.L. RECALLS WHEN OVERALLS SAVED HIS LIFE

Back in the 1920s, an eruption like Vesuvius could not have caused more excitement along Cat Claw Creek than the construction of a new bridge after removal of the old wooden one. Lots of machinery, trucks, stacks of supplies, rebar steel—it was a boyhood paradise of wonderment. However, Mr. Pete and Mrs. Ella were certainly clear to one and all: "*Do not go down there!* It's too dangerous."

Late one afternoon, N.L. was out walking his yo-yo, just kicking up red dust under his feet, and not minding his direction. To his surprise, his wandering had led him (innocent as he was) down to the job site and the skeleton of the new bridge. It was strangely quiet, as the workmen had all gone home and the equipment just sat lifeless, strewn about and laying there. Still, he was working his yo-yo, trying to perfect the around-the-world move when a hand-grabbing miss caused it to soar up and wrap itself around a tree limb like a bola. The tree branch did stick out fairly far, but if he could just shimmy up there and crawl out a way, he could get it back.

His plan was working well in all phases, and he was just about in reach for the yo-yo when a wasp buzzed up and around his head. He swatted and swerved to dodge, became unbalanced, lost his hold, and was sure enough directly over a pit that had iron barbs pointing up to that tree. His overall strap had snagged a stubby stem and there he hung like a puppet—Punch or Judy.

With N.L. looking around, no one was in sight. He looked down at his bare feet swaying over that pit about eight feet below. He could not reach up and was afraid to wiggle much lest the strap break. It was time for prayer! His sister Molly was coming from out behind the barn after spreading chicken pellets and saw the strangest picture away off down the road by the creek. When she went back inside the kitchen door, she said, "Mama, I thought you told us we weren't supposed to go down to that bridge building."

"Yes, that's sure right!" returned Mrs. Ella.

Continued Molly, "Well, I think I just saw N.L. down that way."

"Oh really!" exclaimed Mrs. Ella.

"Yep and he's hanging up in a tree like a monkey or something."

Mrs. Ella only had to holler to Mr. Pete once and, together with Molly in the Model T, they were making a dust trail behind them down that road. When they got there, they had a quick plan, driving the car under the branch. Mrs. Ella exclaimed, "Now you hang on N.L. and you be careful Pete!"

He had already slid up on the roof of the car and was reaching out to the dangling N.L., grabbing him up onto the top of the car as well. Whew!

There was, of course, major relief but no joy riding back home in the silence of the Model T. When they got there, Mr. Pete said, "You know, son, what I have to do." N.L. nodded and turned around.

Mr. Pete took off his waist belt and had one reared back swing and swat when Mrs. Ella cried out, "Do stop Pete, ya'll kill him."

Mr. Pete did stop and, grabbing N.L. by the shoulders, marched him over to his mama, saying, "Here then you raise him!" And that's N.L.'s one and only whipping.

Years later in 1943, Lt. N.L. Tim McLeod was stationed on the army air force base outside Shreveport, Louisiana during the middle of World War II. One day, he was driving a transport truck over a moist, hot, and sticky road in an army issue tee shirt and overalls. All the trucks in one long line had all the windows down for the pathetic whisper of breeze available. Just then he saw it: a large bumble bee that swerved through the open window and dived down inside the left side of his overalls. He could certainly feel the frantic whizzing and buzzing of this invader as he attempted to hand swat him. Every time he took his hold off the wheel, it seemed to have moved to a new anatomic location going south. N.L. had no choice but to force on his brakes, jerk the wheel, and ditch the truck roadside. He tumbled out of the side door, unlatching in any way he could buckles and belts, looking like a man having a seizure in the upright position.

Breathing heavily to get his boots off, he had to single-foot hop half around the truck until there he was in only his BVDs. Yet he never found the bee. MP guards showed up in a hurry and a big burly one yelled out, "Soldier, what in the name of Sam's Hill do you think you are doing?"

N.L. puffed out, "Sir, you see, Sir, this really big bumble bee got into my uniform."

"What?" exclaimed the guard. "You sacrificed the progression of this convoy for a *bee*! Besides I don't see any such thing anywhere. You get dressed and now! You look like a baboon in shorts!"

Lt. N.L. did just that. He reached down to recover his overalls when this really insulted, large bumble bee made his maddest escape—and bee-lined straight up under that MP's chin. Now he was reeling backwards with flailing arms. All N.L. could say under his breath was, "Who's the monkey now," as he joined the parade. He had to smile to himself driving off and thinking, *Just hope the Germans don't shoot bumble bees at us.*

CHAPTER IX

N.L. Gets a New Name

The McLeod farm on Cat Claw Creek was anywhere from one-half to three-quarters of a mile out from Trent, depending on just what it was one was riding upon or in. On a horse as the crow flies, you could cut across pastures and the creek. If N.L. got his chores properly done (his needed inspection from time to time), he could use his weekly allowance riding O'Pepper bareback with a nickel to the pharmacy for a foaming soda and then sit outside on the bench. Just across the main street was the OK Barber Shoppe run by the town's mayor Mr. Wendler.

Now there was an old legend there to assist him with sweeping, toting, and boot cleaning. Everyone called him "Mock," short for moccasin because he was for real an Indian—only one of a tipi full of natives who still remained in that part of west Texas. Legend had it that some of his ancestors were killed up in Palo Duro Canyon by Makenzie's regiment when they slaughtered 1,000 horses in the 1800s.

Mock minded his own business, living just behind the shop in a tiny alley bunkhouse. He had a new window put into his east wall so that at each new day, the sun would rise shining into his lodge. Mock took everything in mild-mannered restraint, even when the little boys would rush around him with finger pistols. But no one bothered his bunk, in the only true alley in town, a short lane of mystery with nooks, crannies, crooks.

One hot day on the drug store bench, N.L saw a commotion starting across the way at the OK. A three-piece-suited cattle buyer and Mock both seemed to trip coming out of the door. With a raised voice, the man said, "Look where you're stepping, you old Comanche. What's wrong with you? Are you drunk!" Turning half around, he yelled back inside, "Is he drunk?"

Mr. Wendler appeared at the door. "Mock, you just need to go on home. We're through for the day." The old Indian stumbled slightly over the plank boardwalk. The buyer had to get in one last comment: "Someone ought to get the sheriff after that old scalper!"

N.L. waited until all had settled down, and he felt drawn to walk across the street to the OK. There he noticed drops of blood on the boards making a small trail, probably from each step that Mock had just made with his right foot. He had to follow the crimson spots down the walk into the alley.

About halfway down was the bunkhouse door, and he could feel his heart beating up between his ears. He did not know whether to just keep following or go get somebody. He moved forward until he came to the bunkroom's little porch and there was Mock's boots. The right one had holes in the sole and was bloody. N.L. did not know if that buyer may have been right and had never seen a drunk man before. He could imagine a bowie knife come flying out of that half-open door.

Something told him to move on with cautious steps up to the door. It was dark inside, but he made Mock out lying on the bunk bed. "Mr. Mock? Mr. Mock, are you all right?" asked N.L.

Mock turned his head to look his direction, saying, "My feet are sick."

N.L. turned and ran around the corner to Mr. Wendler, who was still talking to that buyer. They had both noticed the blood below on the planks. Said the buyer, "See, I told you something's amiss here. Better call the sheriff."

N.L. squeezed past him. "Not the sheriff, Mr. Wendler, better get the doctor. He's bad sick."

Dr. Baker came and very soon it was all threshed out. Mock was immediately sent over to Abilene for surgery and lost all his right toes and half his foot. He had had a diabetic infection and could have died that night without attention. Dr. Baker had been trying for years to treat him, but Mr. Mock always went back to his tribal measures, herbs, and smokes. Dr. Baker surmised that when he tripped going out of the OK that night, it opened the festering sores in his foot.

Word got around about the ol' Indian and his "sugar" illness. Soon he was on his way out of town, going to Oklahoma to live with relatives. But he made one detour south, headed out of Trent about three-quarters of a mile to Cat Claw Creek. Parts of the McLeod family gathered in around the Model T with Mr. Mock spread across the back seat with a bowler hat on his head and washed long hair over his ears.

Mr. Mock pointed one very well-tanned finger at N.L. saying, "To this one that is called N.L. I have nothing to give 'cept my thanks. But also in the hospital the Gideon Bible, they read for me the story of one man older, Paul, being helped by a younger man. So, when I tell my story I too will say I was helped by the younger man that I will now call Timothy!" There was applause and grateful hand waving.

It got to be that "Timothy" was just too formal to say, so it was chopped down to "Tim," which was all right with N.L. Some in the family never forgot that day, but other kinfolk also knew that there was a stubborn mule around there also named Tim. Either way, likeness to a mule verses encounter with a red man, from then on trailing behind like a kite someone might say the name Tim.

After the bombing of Pearl Harbor on December 7, 1941, N.L. and some ACC buddies drove up to Lubbock to enlist in the army. He filled out the papers and handed them to the recruitment officer, who asked what the N.L. stood for.

Replied N.L., "They don't stand for anything. When I was born, I was just given my Dad's initials."

Said the officer, "Well, the initials only will not do. We have to have a name, okay."

N.L. took the papers back, quickly wrote something down, and returned them to the officer, who now said, "That'll do."

When N.L. was finally discharged from the United States Air Force in 1949, he was decommissioned as Captain McLeod, N.L. Tim.

CHAPTER X

N.L. AND THE TRAVELING SALESMAN

One Saturday afternoon late just above Cat Claw Creek, N.L. was stuck on the front porch trying to learn his assignment for school Monday morning: knowing the thirteen original colonies of America. The rest of the family were inside polishing shoes, ironing, reviewing scripture, and getting ready for Sunday services.

N.L. was scratching his head over this "impossible" task when he heard a friendly "Yo" and whistle from the road. In a sprint, a lanky fellow with a tall hat, long coat, and large satchel leaped up on the porch. Doffing his hat, he served a bow with his swing arm, and said, "Sir, I am one Andrew P. McGillacity, take 'cutie' chop off the 'Mc,' discard all together the Andrew P. and I am Gilly for short. Now whom do I have the privilege and pleasure of addressing here—whereas I can surmise a young scholar with your book?"

N.L. sat stunned for the next millennium, having never been

peppered at such close range with a shotgun blast of words like this before. Finally, he got his head bearings back and said, "I am N.L. and I have to know the thirteen colonies by Monday."

Said the salesman, "Splendid! Why there's nothing to it for a lad of your caliber."

About this time, Mrs. Ella was shouting through the house, "Who you'd be talking to out there?" Simultaneously opening the front door, she saw for herself another traveling salesman.

Gilly did not break cadence, and with long-fingered dexterity, he gracefully extended his hand and politely caught hers. "And you ma'am are the ever bustling Mrs. McLeod that the neighbors all remarked about and I am so honored to greet you now. I presume Mr. McLeod and children are hereabouts? May I meet them all?"

Directly the front porch was loaded and Ella pronounced down the line all their names ending up with, "And this is Pete my husband."

Gilly looked bright-eyed over the collection. Then, in quick step, he started at the top of the line with a brisk handshake and gave each one back his name until finally coming down to "Mr. McLeod—Pete." Everyone stood in disbelief, knowing that at times Mr. Pete and Mrs. Ella could not remember who was who much less a total stranger.

With another wave of his hand, he said, "All easily explained. I had to but remember this boy's name Delmer, whose twin Elmer I envisioned charring some Spam, no less and at home. That gave me char for Charelton, Spam for Sam, no less for N.L., and of course home for Homer. For the lovely girls, I recalled Bea-utea-iful b-Beatrice, e-Ethel, a-Asha, and English tea is jolly good, therefore Molly, and a cup of joe for Joe-Ella." You could hear the collective drop of a dozen jaws.

Now Gilly went right to work with his audience already won over. He opened his satchel and scarfs and sweet-smelling boxes came tumbling out with all sorts of kitchen ware. All the smaller kids got sticks of bubble gum, the girls little hankies, Mrs. Ella a new egg-beater spoon, boys together a domino set, Mr. Pete the shave brush, and for Mr. Gilly's pocket a collection of coins up to five dollars.

One last item as he was gathering up to leave was to quiz N.L. on his homework.

"Too hard!" exclaimed N.L.

Returned the salesman, "Sure, if you have a bird's nest for a brain *but* my dear boy I can tell you have a noggin for thoughts not twigs. Why, I can show you a method known only by me and sultans of Araby. Now listen fast. Let's see—thirteen colonies?" He turned with a finger pointed skyward.

"Okay, Homer, cut me a strand horse hair from the neck. Delmer, I need a large jar." He went on assigning something for each to go and fetch back: safety pin, Band-Aids, crayons, cow's tooth, vinegar label, a snip off your dad's old long johns, a fork, a piece of ham bone, a ring, a chocolate label, and a swipe of dust off your road. When all was brought together, he looked N.L. in the eye and said, "Now listen faster!"

Monday morning came, with N.L. ahead of the first of ray of morning light. There was an eternity inside an eternity until he was finally seated in class before his teacher. The teacher, with some bemusement, asked N.L. if he knew his assignment. With his collection in the jar, N.L. proceeded to the front and the presentation table. Taking a deep sigh, he launched out.

"The thirteen colonies." He paused. "Well, this is my jar for Georgia; my two crayons for Carolinas North and South; two labels one sticky syrup and one vinegar for Vermont,and Virginia; a ring for marriage like in Maryland; the fork—New York; horse hair from the mane for Maine; patch of my dad's underwear for Delaware; safety pin for Pennsylvania; cow tooth—only one state has a tooth in it: Massachusetts; one Band-Aid for cuts—Connecticut; Hershey label for Jersey as in New Jersey; a pig's bone, which is ham bone, for New Hampshire." Finally, with flair, he emptied the jar. "And road dust for Rhode Island, and there you have it—all thirteen!"

The class exploded into applause and as the accolades slowly died down, the teacher asked, "How ever did you learn to do all that?"

N.L. just grinned and said, "A sultan from Araby taught me."

CHAPTER XI

N.L. LEARNS A LESSON ABOUT PARENTS

N.L. did not have to cross Cat Claw Creek and go to school until his eighth birthday. Mrs. Ella kept him home as long as she could, he being the last of her eleven children. He had to pay his dues getting over a little teasing from the regular boys. Finally, being the last at bat so many times and getting to peek through a peephole into the girl's locker room only after all the girls were already gone, he was beginning to fit astride.

One topic that was continually broadcast was the heroics and horrors of fathers and uncles in World War I and who got medals, who bombed this and that, saved France, and swung their rifles like David Crockett over the Kaiser. What N.L. had not fully filtered through was the chance for "whopperness" that could blow up any tale like a face covered with bubble gum.

N.L. could not recall any such stories for his own dad in the "war to end all wars." As it happened, there was an evening when Mr. Pete had the Model T in town and was giving him a ride back home.

N.L. asked, "Dad, you weren't no army man in the war?"

"Nope," returned Mr. Pete.

Continued N.L., "So you didn't do nothing to stop the Germans?"

Very factually again, Mr. Pete said, "Reckon not, on the battlefield."

"So you just stayed home all those war years?"

"True, you might say that."

The rest of the ride home was all silence between father and son. When N.L. got out of the car, he played a little around the yard until he had to check up on his one and only job, and that was to be sure all the water troughs were filled up. Supper came with the usual chorus of small talk. Only, Mr. Pete seemed a little more quiet than usual and did not even ask anybody to light his pipe for him but did it himself.

That night, N.L., in pajamas, expected one of his parents to come up to his loft and tuck the covers. Mrs. Ella came and this time she sat down on the bed.

"I want to talk with you just a minute about what you and Pete talked about coming home today. I'll be quiet 'cause he doesn't want me saying anything about it up here anyway. When we got into that war in '17, your Daddy was over thirty years old, and it may not be right, but it's young men, nineteen or twenty who go off to war. Plus, he was raising all our kids and running this farm. What he did do was raise crops for the army. Eatin' is mighty important to an army—food to fight, they say. He used mules again so the army could have tractors. He saved metal and volunteered to search the dump yards for old tires and wire. Also, your Daddy and I visited the few families in these parts that weren't going to get their son or brother back home, 'cause they were killed, you see. We prayed to God to save

42

souls at home and over seas. Like our preacher said, the front just ain't were bullets fly and bombs go off; it's all the way back were where we support these men. I promise I ain't knowed any one soldier that didn't want to only do his duty and light back for home. Your Daddy never carried a rifle but he carried the rightness of the cause in his heart. Some men wear steel helmets, others just as good—they wear straw hats and farm. Think you understand now a little better about your daddy? Now you sleep tight—no bed bugs bite." She leaned over and kissed his forehead.

Breakfast that next morning was the usual platters of eggs, biscuits, ham, jams and butter, and, of course, Mr. Pete sitting there at the head of the table. When N.L. came in, he stopped alongside and looked at Pete like it was the first time he actually really *saw* him, those brown, deep farmer lines etching his brow, cheeks, his neck.

"Dad I, au, I."

Mr. Pete patted his shoulder. "Get around there and get your breakfast."

"Well, I just think a lot of you feeding the army the way you did."

Mr. Pete laughed. "Yes, well I had good practice with this little battalion we have right here."